IF YOU CAN'T "BEAR HUG, AIR HUG"

A book inspired by social distancing

by
Katie Sedmak

ISBN: 978-0-578-70067-0 (paperback)

Published by Pink Pangolin LLC
2020 Howell Mill Road NW, Suite D-101
Atlanta, GA 30318-1732

www.theairhugbook.com | @theairhugbook | theairhugbook

A Letter to Parents and Educators

Thanks so much for adding "If You Can't Bear Hug, Air Hug" to your collection. I hope you and your little ones enjoy it.

Love can be difficult enough to express in ideal circumstances; it becomes even more challenging when keeping six feet apart. That's what drove me to create this book. I want children (and adults) to see that there are many ways to express love without touching, and to reassure children that they are loved even when they can't be physically close to others.

"If You Can't Bear Hug, Air Hug" is intended to be a tool for you. This book will inspire your child with fun ways to bond while distancing. From there, it opens a door for you to have as simple or as complex of a conversation about COVID-19 as you deem appropriate for your child.

I hope this book uplifts you and the child you care about. I know we can get through this, and even share some fun and laughter along the way.

Life After 2020, a Series on Community Mental Health. This item is part of our grant from ALA & ARSL.

LIBRARIES TRANSFORMING COMMUNITIES
FOCUS ON SMALL AND RURAL LIBRARIES

A SPECIAL GRANT FOR SMALL AND RURAL COMMUNITIES

AWARD RECIPIENT

— Katie

Katie Sedmak, Author & Illustrator

Dedicated to my family, with big air hugs.

If you can't **bear hug,**
air hug.

Smiling snouts, fuzzy bellies out,
we stretch our arms out wide.

If you can't **slap fins,**
flash grins.

Eyes twinkling, cheeks dimpling,
we show off our enormous teeth.

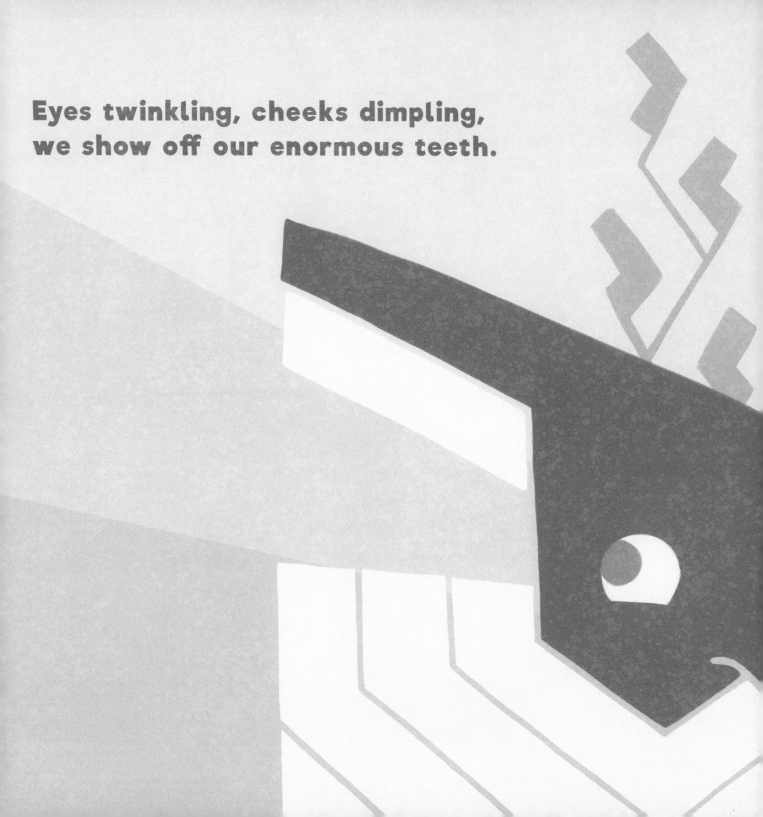

If you can't **bump knuckles,
trade chuckles.**

Quiet giggling,
seashells wiggling,
we share jokes late at night.

If you can't **tickle feathers,**
sing together.

Talons tapping,
wings flapping,
we "hoo,
      hoo,
           hoo" in rhythm.

If you can't **split a fish,**
share a wish.

Fluffy heads on floating beds,
we spot a shooting star.

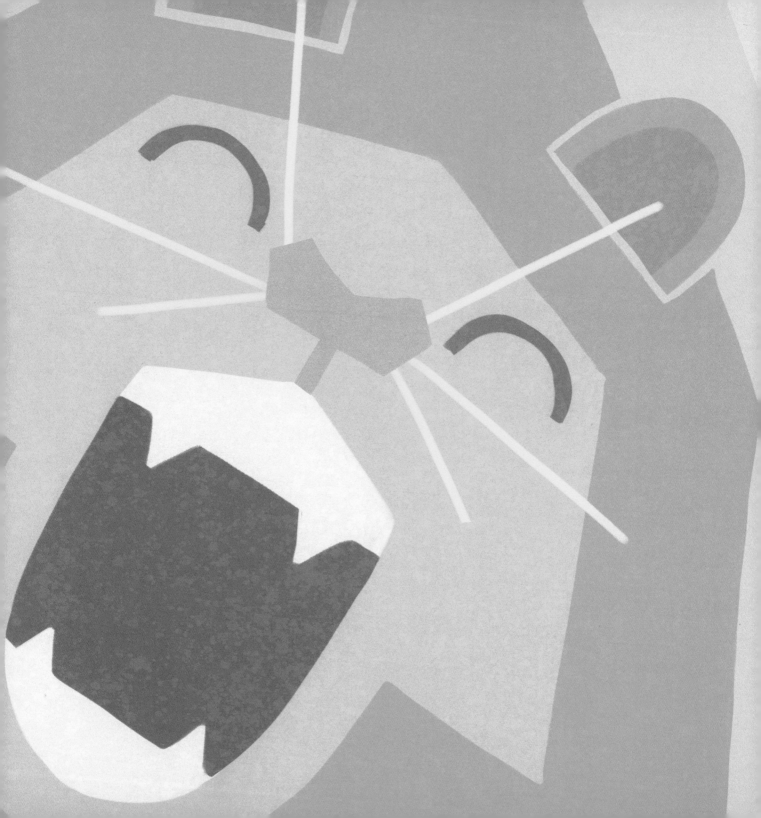

If you can't
share **snores**,
share **roars.**

Chests puffed, manes fluffed,
we see who growls the loudest.

If you can't **touch noses,** give roses.

Trunks twisting, tails swishing,
we pick a perfect bloom.

If you can't **rub whiskers**,
be good **listeners.**

Heads perked, ears alert,
we have a heart-to-heart.

If you can't **give pecks,**
rain **check.**

Chirping our songs,
we say "so long!"
and wave our wings 'til then.

If you can't **share bamboo,**
share a view.

Sleepy eyes on colorful skies,
we watch the sun go down.

the
end